A NOTE TO PARENTS

Reading Aloud with Your Child

Research shows that reading books aloud is the single most valuable support parents can provide in helping children learn to read.

- Be a ham! The more enthusiasm you display, the more your child will enjoy the book.
- Run your finger underneath the words as you read to signal that the print carries the story.
- Leave time for examining the illustrations more closely; encourage your child to find things in the pictures.
- Invite your youngster to join in whenever there's a repeated phrase in the text.
- Link up events in the book with similar events in your child's life.
- If your child asks a question, stop and answer it. The book can be a means to learning more about your child's thoughts.

Listening to Your Child Read Aloud

The support of your attention and praise is absolutely crucial to your child's continuing efforts to learn to read.

- If your child is learning to read and asks for a word, give it immediately so that the meaning of the story is not interrupted. DO NOT ask your child to sound out the word.
- On the other hand, if your child initiates the act of sounding out, don't intervene.
- If your child is reading along and makes what is called a miscue, listen for the sense of the miscue. If the word "road" is substituted for the word "street," for instance, no meaning is lost. Don't stop the reading for a correction.
- If the miscue makes no sense (for example, "horse" for "house"), ask your child to reread the sentence because you're not sure you understand what's just been read.
- Above all else, enjoy your child's growing command of print and make sure you give lots of praise. *You are your child's first teacher—and the most important one. Praise from you is critical for further risk-taking and learning.*

—Priscilla Lynch
Ph.D., New York University
Educational Consultant

For Julian
—T.J.

For my friends Lucy, Gretchen, and Anna
—A.B.

Library of Congress Cataloging-in-Publication Data

Johnston, Tony.
We love the dirt / by Tony Johnston; illustrated by Alexa Brandenberg.
p. cm. —(Hello reader! Level 1)
Summary: The people, animals, and objects on the farm explain their relationship with the dirt, which is used and needed by all.
ISBN 0-590-92953-4
[1. Farm life —Fiction. 2. Soils —Fiction.] I. Brandenberg, Alexa, ill. II. Title. III. Series.
PZ7.J6478We 1997
[E]—dc20 96-10588
CIP
AC

12 11 10 9 0 1 2/0

Printed in the U.S.A. 24

First Scholastic printing, April 1997

We Love the Dirt

by Tony Johnston
Illustrated by Alexa Brandenberg

Hello Reader! — Level 1

SCHOLASTIC INC.
New York Toronto London Auckland Sydney

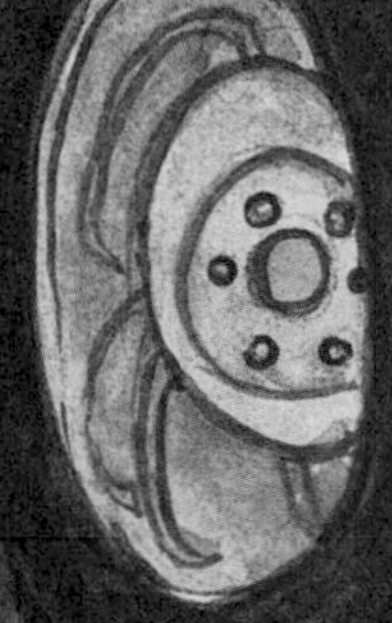

I am the farmer.
I wear a red shirt.
I am the farmer.
I plow the dirt.

I am the mother.
I wear a big hat.
I am the mother.
I weed the dirt.

I am the sister.
I make the dessert.
I am the sister.
I squish the dirt.

I am the baby.
I grow spurt by spurt.

I am the baby.
I taste the dirt.

I am the water.
I squirt and I squirt.
I am the water.
I wet the dirt.

am the pig.
snuffle and snort.
am the pig.
wear the dirt.

I am the chicken
I travel barefoot.
I am the chicken.
I peck the dirt.

I am the cat.
I clean my fur coat.
I am the cat.
I hate the dirt.

I am the toad.
I'm warty and short.
I am the toad.
I hop in the dirt.

I am the worm.
I live in the grit.
I am the worm.
I turn the dirt.

I am the seed.
I sleep or I sprout.
I am the seed.
I grow in the dirt.

I am the wheat.
I whisper a lot.
I am the wheat.
My feet are dirt.

I am the scarecrow.
I am brave and alert.
I am the scarecrow.
I guard the dirt.

I am the tree.
I hold my arms out.
I am the tree.
I shade the dirt.

I am the flower.
I grow where I want.
I am the flower.
I grace the dirt.

I am the star.
I have a bright heart.
I am the star.
I light the dirt.

I am the cricket.
I tiptoe unheard.
I am the cricket.
I sing to dirt.

I am the barn owl.
I go out at night.
I am the barn owl.
I scout the dirt.

I am the field.
I look like a quilt.
I am the field.
I *am* the dirt.

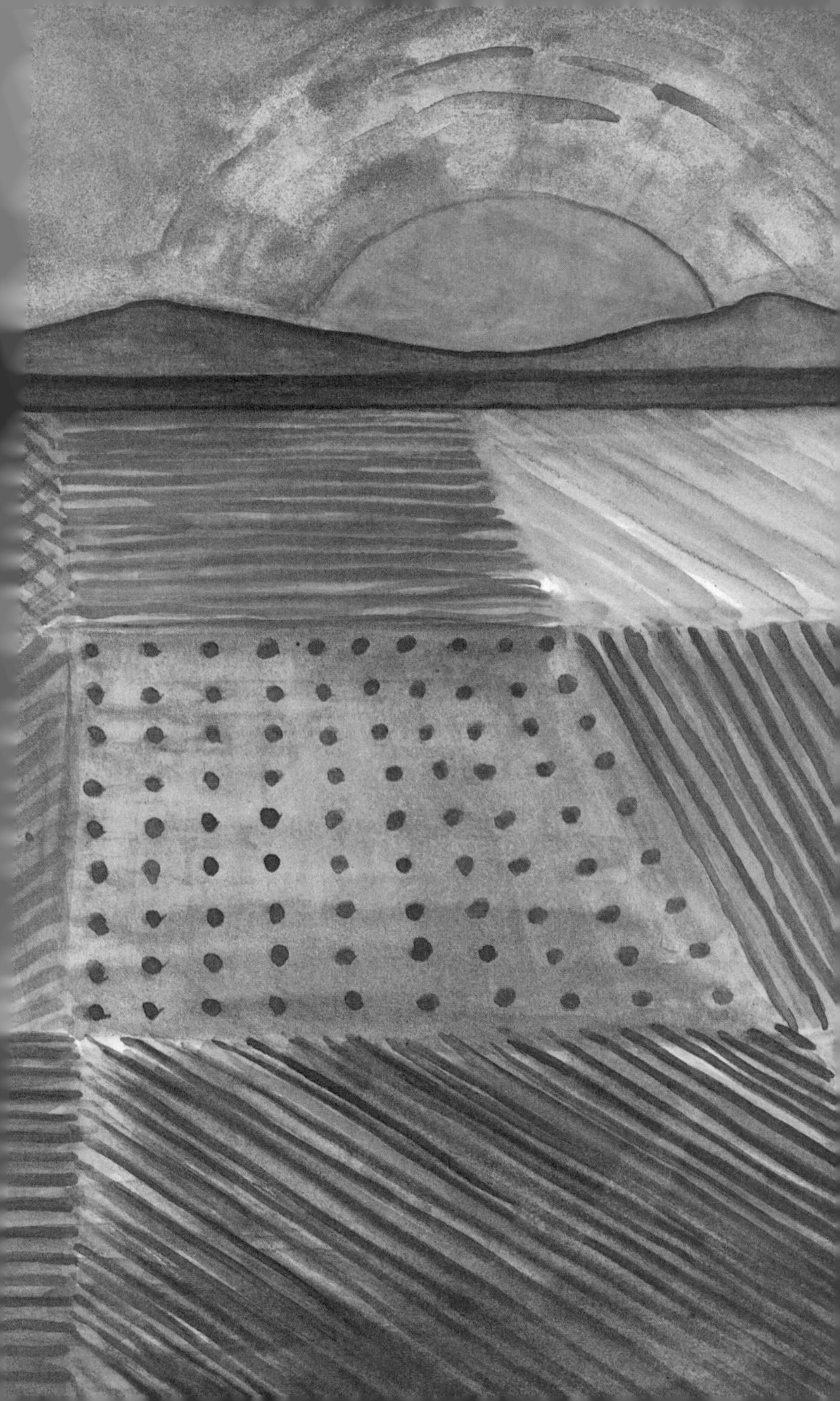

We are the farm.
We all are it.

We are the farm.
We love the dirt.

(Except for the cat.)
And that is that.